DiBS!

For Nathan,
who called
dibs on this
book,
with all my
love
—L.G.

For all my
children who
always call
dibs on me :)
—M.P.

Carolrhoda Books
A division of Lerner Publishing Group, Inc.
241 First Avenue North
Minneapolis, MN 55401 USA

For reading levels and more information, look up this title at www.lernerbooks.com.

Starry background by Social Media Hub/Shutterstock.com.

Designed by Kimberly Morales.
Main body text set in Chaloops Medium 19/24. Typeface provided by Chank.
The illustrations in this book were created with Photoshop, Painter, and Procreate.

Library of Congress Cataloging-in-Publication Data

Names: Gehl, Laura, author. | Piwowarski, Marcin, illustrator.
Title: Dibs / by Laura Gehl ; [illustrated by Marcin Piwowarski].
Description: Minneapolis : Carolrhoda Books, [2019] | Summary: When baby Clancy's first word is "dibs," his older brother, Julian, is not pleased, especially as Clancy claims their parents' bed, the White House, and even a rocket ship.
Identifiers: LCCN 2018006982 (print) | LCCN 2018014349 (ebook) | ISBN 9781541541795 (eb pdf) | ISBN 9781512465327 (lb : alk. paper)
Subjects: | CYAC: Belongings, Personal—Fiction. | Brothers—Fiction. | Family life—Fiction. | Humorous stories.
Classification: LCC PZ7.G2588 (ebook) | LCC PZ7.G2588 Dib 2019 (print) | DDC [E]—dc23

LC record available at https://lccn.loc.gov/2018006982

Manufactured in the United States of America
1-43064-32221-7/18/2018

DIBS!

Laura Gehl

illustrated by **Marcin Piwowarski**

Carolrhoda Books • Minneapolis

When Julian wanted something, he always called DiBS.

"Dibs on the solar system plate!"

Clancy watched and learned. And one day Clancy said his first word.

But that was just the beginning.

Soon, Clancy called dibs on his parents' bed.

Then Clancy called dibs on the bakery.

And on an airplane.

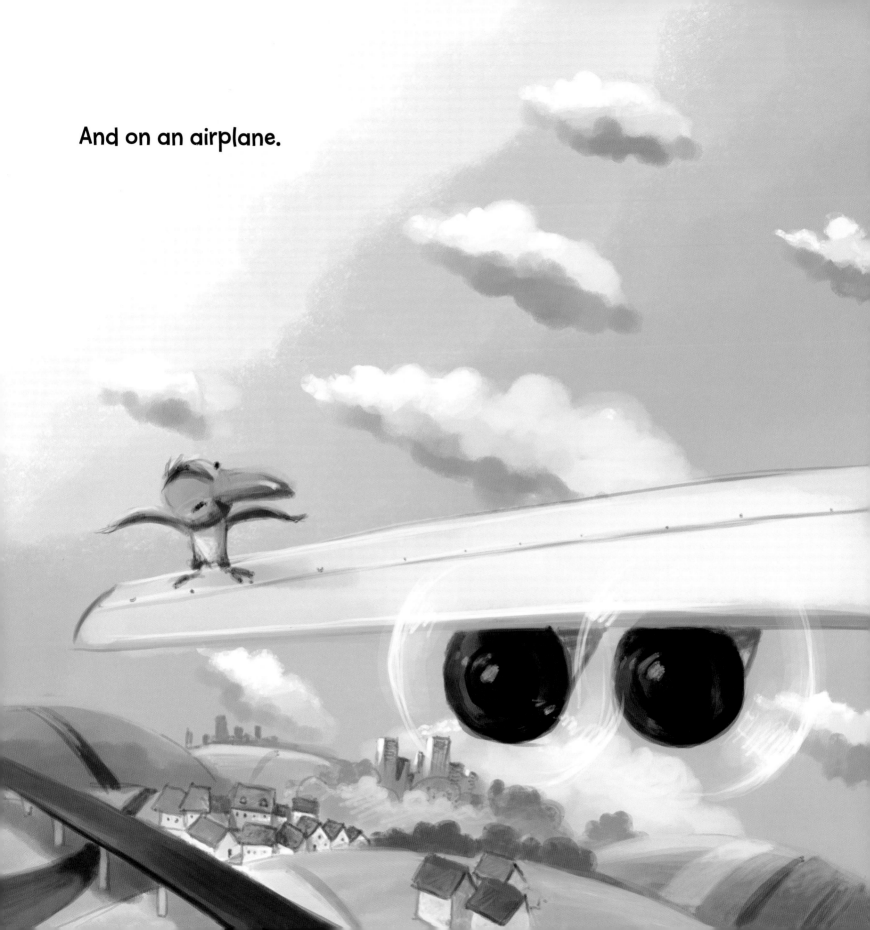

Julian tried to tell everyone that dibs didn't work like that.

"You can call dibs on the biggest piece of cake, but not on a whole bakery.

"You can call dibs on a toy airplane, but not on a real airplane.

"And you can't call dibs on the White House! You need to be elected!"

But nobody listened to Julian.

Not Mom.

Not Dad.

And definitely not Clancy.

So when Clancy called dibs on NASA and blasted off, Julian said, "I hope you stay in space for a long, long time!"

Back at home, Julian had the toys all to himself.

He had the cookies all to himself.

And he had his parents all to himself.

Except that Clancy *did* stay in space for a long, long time. A lot longer than Julian had expected.

And Julian started to worry.
What if Clancy was lost?
What if Clancy needed help?

Julian marched into his favorite museum.

Julian blasted into space to search for Clancy.

"You can't have the rocket," the aliens told Julian. "We called dibs."

"You can keep the rocket," agreed Julian.
"But I call dibs too."

It was surprisingly difficult to point a finger
while wearing a space suit. But Julian managed.

It was also surprisingly difficult to hug a little brother
while wearing a space suit. But Julian managed.

Once Clancy was safely inside Julian's rocket ship, both brothers realized how hungry space travel had made them.